Satchelmouse

and

THE DOLL'S HOUSE

Written by Antonia Barber

Illustrated by Claudio Muñoz

BARRON'S

NEW YORK

W9-AWK-876

The village school had a big doll's house.

It had once belonged to an old lady who lived nearby.

The old lady had played with it when she was a little girl.

Sarah thought the doll's house was beautiful.

She liked the four-poster bed with its pink silk covers.

She liked the pretty curving staircase with the red carpet.

She liked the tiny china dishes on the dining room table.

She liked the shiny black stove in the basement kitchen.

For the children of
Appledore School
A.B.

For my mother
C.M.

First edition for the United States published 1988 by
Barron's Educational Series, Inc.

First published 1987 by Walker Books Ltd., London, England

Text © Copyright 1987 Antonia Barber
Illustrations © Copyright 1987 Claudio Muñoz

All rights reserved. No part of this book may be reproduced
in any form, by photostat, microfilm, xerography, or any
other means, or incorporated into any information
retrieval system, electronic or mechanical, without
the written permission of the copyright owner.

All inquiries should be addressed to:
Barron's Educational Series, Inc.
250 Wireless Boulevard, Hauppauge, NY 11788

Library of Congress Cataloging-in-Publication Data
Barber, Antonia, 1932-
Satchelmouse and the doll's house.
Summary: Admiring the dolls in a dollhouse, Sarah is
transformed into the servant doll through the magic
spell of a mischievous mouse.
[1. Dolls–Fiction.   2. Household employees–Fiction.
3. Magic–Fiction]   I. Muñoz, Claudio, ill.   II. Title.
PZ7.B2323Sat   1988   [E]   87-14340
ISBN 0-8120-5873-9

Printed in Italy
789   9685   987654321

The doll's house had a family of dolls who lived upstairs.

The family had a lot of servants who lived downstairs.

"Which of the dolls would you like to be?" Mrs. James asked the children.

"I'd like to be the father," said Darren. The father had sideburns and looked very important.

"I want to be the cook," said Jenny, who liked to play with the tiny pots and pans.

"I'd be the butler," said Mark, "and taste all the lovely food."

"I'd like to be the little girl," said Sarah.

The little girl had rosy cheeks and a white dress. She sat at a frilly dressing table. She slept in the four-poster bed.

Sarah's friend Satchelmouse was listening. He was a tall brown mouse in a red jacket. Inside the jacket was a pencil case full of useful things. The pencil sharpener was a golden trumpet and only Sarah knew that it had magic powers.

"Do you really want to be the little girl?" asked Satchelmouse.

"Oh, yes, please!" said Sarah. She was looking at the rosebuds on the white dress.

She did not notice that Satchelmouse was smiling to himself.

He picked up the magic trumpet and began to play.

Sarah grew smaller and smaller.

She found herself in the pretty bedroom standing beside the four-poster bed.

She hurried over to the dressing table to look at herself in the mirror... but she saw to her horror that she was a little *servant* girl in a cap and apron!

The bedroom door flew open and in came
the girl in the white dress.
Her rosy face looked very bad tempered.
"Stop admiring yourself in my mirror,"
she told Sarah crossly, "and make my bed."
Making a four-poster bed was not easy.
Sarah was quite out of breath when
she had finished.
"Now get back downstairs,
where you belong," said the doll
in the white dress.

As Sarah went down the pretty curving staircase, she met the father coming up.

"This carpet is very dusty!" he said. "Clean it at once!"

It took a long time to brush the red carpet. Sarah grew hot and dirty.

"This is all your fault, Satchelmouse," she protested. "You knew I wanted to be the girl in the white dress."

"You only said 'the little girl'," Satchelmouse pointed out.

"But I didn't even notice the little servant girl," explained Sarah.

"Nobody ever does," said Satchelmouse.

The butler came out of the dining room with a tray of dirty dishes. "Take these to the kitchen," he said, "and wash them."

When Sarah had finished those dishes, the butler brought more dirty dishes.

By the time they were all done, Sarah felt tired and greasy.

The cook came bustling in.
"If you've finished washing up, you
can polish the stove," she said.
When Sarah complained, the cook
chased her around the kitchen
with a rolling pin.

It took so long to make the stove clean and shiny! Sarah's face and hands were covered with black polish.

"Magic me back to the classroom, Satchelmouse," she begged, "before they find any more work for me to do!"

"Poor Sarah," said Satchelmouse, trying hard not to laugh.

He played a cheerful tune and Sarah
began to grow again.

Soon she was back outside the doll's
house, looking in.

Sarah found the little servant doll
behind the table in the kitchen.

She was out of sight,
scrubbing the floor.

When no one was looking, Sarah took off the doll's cap and apron and dressed her in the white dress.

She laid her on the four-poster bed. "You need a good rest!" she told her.

Then Sarah dressed the rosy-cheeked doll
in the cap and apron and put her
in the kitchen.

"See how *you* like it!" she said.